I NEED U

NOW & FOREVER

KRISHNA BHARATHI S A

Made with ♥ on the Notion Press Platform
www.notionpress.com

To the one I love!

Contents

Preface

Hello here! I hope that your day went better than yesterday and that you are in the perfect mood to read my book right now. I am Krishna Bharathi S A, an unstoppable aspirant who believes in causation theory. I have valuable insights from my journey as a writer, but it would be a separate book if I started to write. So it's best if I stick to the content that I'm interested in. Whenever I begin to write a book myself, the very first thing I focus on is the core content itself. Also, I had always dreamed of writing a book in a single sentence, irrespective of its size or number of pages. And I wanted to write to everyone to tell them how much I loved them. This book served as an opportunity to do so. Despite its size and the number of pages, this book is comprised of several backstories and flashbacks that I can connect with, and it is truly a piece of memory for me. This book is a love story that explores the ups and downs of romantic relationships while also serving as a heartfelt letter to my loved ones. With its powerful narrative and thought-provoking insights, this book will touch your soul and challenge your perceptions of love. The pages within this book offer a journey into the depths of the human experience, where you will find yourself reflecting on your own relationships and the role they play in your life. And through this book, I do write that my love for my loved ones cannot be expressed in words and that I wanted to tell them, "I need U!"

Dad! I Love You!

Dad! I love you! From the moment I was born, you have been there for me, guiding me through life and providing me with a never-ending source of love. Your unwavering devotion to our family and your selfless acts of kindness towards others inspire me every day. Your gentle touch and warm embrace have provided me with comfort and happiness in even the darkest of times. You have always been my safe haven and my closest confidant. Your unwavering love and support have given me the courage and strength to face any challenges that come my way. You have taught me so much throughout my life, imparting your wisdom, guidance, and values, which have shaped me into the person I am today. I have learned so much from you about life and what it means to be a good person. I am also thankful for the memories we have shared, the adventures we have been on and the laughter we have shared. I love you more than words can express and I will always be here for you, no matter what happens. I need you! Now and forever!

Mom! I Love You!

Mom! I love you! You are the light of my life, the one who has always been there for me through thick and thin. Growing up, I always felt like the luckiest kid in the world because I had the best mother. Every morning, you would wake up early to make me breakfast and pack my lunch for school. You would tuck me in at night and listen to me as I rambled on about my day. Even as I grew older and became more independent, you were always there for me, offering a listening ear, a shoulder to cry on, and wise advice. Your love is unconditional, and I know that no matter what I do, you'll always be there for me. You have always put my needs before your own, sacrificing so much just to give me the best life possible. From your selfless acts of kindness to your unwavering support, you have shown me the true meaning of love. You are my hero and I admire your strength and resilience, especially in the face of adversity. You have overcome so much in your life, and yet you never give up. Your courage and determination inspire me to be a better person every day. My love for you is immeasurable, and it only continues to grow stronger with each passing day. I love you more than words can express and I will always be here for you, no matter what happens. I need you! Now and forever!

Sister! I Love You!

Sister! I love you! You have been a constant source of joy and comfort in my life and I can never thank you enough for the love and care you have showered upon me. I still remember the day you were born and how our parents brought you home wrapped in a soft pink blanket. You were so tiny and delicate and I felt a rush of excitement and love for this new addition to our family. As you grew up, I watched in amazement as you developed your own unique personality full of energy. Your infectious laugh and wide grin have always brought a smile to my face and I cherish the moments we've spent together. Your achievements, big and small, never cease to amaze me and I am always in awe of your determination and drive to succeed. I also appreciate the way you have always stood by my side even when I have made mistakes or let you down. In so many ways, you have shaped the person I am today and I am forever grateful for your love and influence in my life. I promise that we will continue to grow and strengthen our bond in the years to come and that our love will only continue to flourish. I love you more than words can express and I will always be here for you, no matter what happens. I need you! Now and forever!

CHAPTER ONE

I Need U!

Back when tigers smoked, there stood a great empire where mighty armies marched to conquer its wealth and yet remained undefeated, the rulers and their subjects were equally devoted to the arts filling their cities with stunning artworks that showcased their passion for beauty inspiring generations of artists to push the boundaries of their talents and leave behind a legacy of culture and imagination that would endure for centuries ruled by a visionary ruler who understood the power of the arts to unite his subjects, inspire his armies to elevate the prestige of his kingdom, and so he devoted himself to fostering the arts sponsoring lavish competitions that brought the finest artists from across the land to showcase their talents commissioning grandiose works of art that would rival the greatest masterpieces of the ancient world, personally studying the arts immersing himself in their beauty and wisdom emerging as a patron and practitioner of the arts earning the affection of his people especially the queen, the king's beloved wife was the shining light of the royal court, her grace and elegance inspiring all who met her, her charity and kindness warming the hearts of the people and her love for her children, the crown prince was the hope of the kingdom, his intelligence and charisma belying his youth and showing the promise of a great leader, his curiosity and adventurous spirit led him to explore the far corners of the empire and beyond, learning from its people and his love of the arts shining through in his talents as an artist captivating audiences with his performances and earning him the admiration of the court, but his greatest strength was his compassion and empathy, his unwavering commitment to justice and fairness and his devotion to his family especially his younger sibling, the princess was a vision of beauty and kindness, her soft smile and gentle laughter bringing joy to all who met her, her love for art and nature captivating all who heard her play or saw her wander through the gardens and her charitable spirit and unwavering commitment to justice earned her the admiration of the people and the respect of the court, but despite the privileges and pressures of her rank driven by a deep passion for the arts was always eager to expand her knowledge and push the boundaries of her creativity and so when she heard of a rare and mysterious form of art that was said to bring enlightenment and harmony to those who mastered it, she was determined to learn it embarking on a journey of discovery,facing challenges and obstacles along the way, but never losing her resolve made the bold decision to disguise herself as a commoner and enrol in the prestigious School of Arts where she lived and studied alongside the most talented artists of the kingdom learning from the best challenging herself to grow and forming deep and meaningful connections with her mates, while a commoner, humble and hardworking was just going about his daily life pursuing his passion for the arts and dreaming of making a name for himself in the world when he caught a glimpse of the princess disguised as a fellow student and was struck by her beauty feeling a deep and undeniable connection to her in that moment, despite the danger and impossibility of a commoner and a princess being together, he found himself unable to resist the pull of his heart driven by his shy but sincere interest in the princess struggled to find the courage to speak to her often finding himself tongue-tied and awkward in her presence, but determined to make a connection and hopefully become friends, he practiced what he would say, studied her interests and hobbies and finally mustered up the nerve to approach her nervously starting a conversation about her art hoping to impress her with his knowledge and show her his own passion for the arts, but despite his best efforts, he found himself stumbling over his words and failing to make a strong impression feeling discouraged and ready to give up, but then to his surprise she smiled warmly at him sparking a conversation that lasted for hours, they shared love of the arts and their mutual admiration for each other's talents breaking down the barriers between them and setting the stage for a friendship that would change both of their lives forever threw himself into learning everything he could about her listening to her stories sharing his own and helping her navigate the complexities of life at the School of Arts and beyond showing her kindness and support through every challenge and triumph and as they grew closer, they found themselves confiding in each other discussing their hopes and fears and forming a bond that was unbreakable and unshakable and the commoner realising the depth and intensity of his feelings for the princess, no longer able to deny the truth of his heart began to prepare himself for the ultimate expression of his love knowing that this was the moment that would determine the course of his life and his future with the woman he loved and so he gathered his courage practised what he would say selected the perfect setting and the perfect moment made his way to her, but was suddenly struck by tragedy when the princess went missing from the School of Arts and he searched for her visiting every class and every studio scouring the campus and the surrounding town asking everyone he encountered for any information or clues about her whereabouts, he found himself growing more and more desperate and devastated as each lead turned out to be a dead end and each day without her seemed like an eternity, his mind racing with all the worst-case scenarios and his heart aching with fear and sorrow until finally he received a message that would shatter his world revealing the truth of her disappearance and the reasons behind it forcing him to confront the fact that he may have lost the love of his life and that his future which had once seemed so bright was now filled with uncertainty and heartbreak causing him to question everything he thought he knew and everything he had once held and leaving him struggling to find meaning and purpose in a world without her, but to his surprise the princess returned to the School of Arts revealing her true identity as the crown princess of the kingdom accompanied by a guard of soldiers and the commoner filled with hope and determination took a step towards the princess when his heart overflowing with love and his eyes shining with joy, but as he approached her, he was stopped by her guards who barred his way with their swords and their armor and as he looked into their steely eyes, he realized that his love for her was not enough that he was still just a commoner and she was still a princess that their worlds were still as far apart as they ever were as he turned away his heart heavy and his spirit broken, he felt himself crumbled and overwhelmed by the weight of his sadness and his weakness and as he stumbled he was caught by his friends who helped him to his feet and whispered words of comfort in his ear, but no matter how much they tried they could not ease the pain of his loss, his heart shattered and his soul empty wandering aimlessly through the streets lost in his grief and his despair until he found himself at the edge of the kingdom as he gazed out at the endless horizon, he realised that he could go no further that he had reached the end of his journey and that he could not go on without her who had once been filled with hope and love was now consumed by anger and bitterness as he watched the princess change before his very eyes becoming distant and cold and turning against him no longer the warm and loving woman he had known, despite his anger and bitterness towards the princess the commoner found himself unable to leave the School of Arts where he had once been so happy and content drawn back by the memories of all the good times he had shared with the other students and teachers and the passion he had once felt for learning and creating as he tried to continue his studies in secret, he found that his hatred for the princess only grew stronger as he saw her abuse her power and treat the other students and teachers with cruelty and disdain and despite all his best efforts to ignore her and stay out of her way, she continued to find ways to hurt him and make his life miserable either directly or through her loyal followers, but still he persevered and determined to prove to himself and to everyone else that he was just as worthy and capable as she was, he found that he was becoming more and more skilled and accomplished and he saw the looks of admiration and respect from his classmates, he felt his confidence and self-esteem grow and even as he continued to clash with the princess and her followers, he felt a deep sense of satisfaction and fulfillment knowing that he was no longer the weak and helpless commoner he had once been, but a strong and capable artist who had overcome all the obstacles life had thrown in his path and one day the commoner's anger and bitterness towards the princess slowly began to dissipate as he began to see her in a different light as he learned the truth about her life and the pressures she faced as a princess and as he saw how she struggled to balance her duties as a ruler with her own desires and needs, he began to understand why she had acted the way she did and as he saw her vulnerable and her kindness towards those in need, he realized that she was not the cruel and selfish person he had thought she was but a complex and multifaceted individual who was just as human as he was and as he began to forgive her and let go of his anger, he felt his love for her rekindle and he found himself once again drawn to her despite all the obstacles that lay between them and as he approached her hoping to mend their relationship, he found that she was just as eager to reconcile and as they stood before each other, he felt their eyes meet and he saw the love and the longing in her gaze and he knew that despite all the challenges they faced, they were meant to be together and as he took her hand and pulled her close, he felt her warm embrace and he whispered his love for her into her ear and as he looked into her eyes, he saw the tears of happiness and relief and he knew that he had finally found the happiness he had been seeking all along and as they stood together with their love and their passion for art, they knew that they were destined to conquer the obstacles life would throw in their path and that they would always be together now and forever.

Hey! I Love You!

Hey! I love you! You have brought so much joy and light into my life and every day I am grateful for your presence in it. Your smile brightens up my day and the sound of your laughter fills me with a happiness that I never knew existed. Your touch sends shivers down my spine and I feel so safe and loved in your arms. Your love is a treasure beyond measure and I am humbled to have been blessed with it. Your unwavering support and encouragement even in the toughest of times is a testament to the strength of our love. You have a heart of gold and I am so grateful to have you as my partner in life. Every moment spent with you is a moment that I will always cherish. Your embrace is like a warm blanket on a cold day and your laughter is like music to my ears. Your eyes, they hold a twinkle that sets my soul on fire. Your beauty, both inside and out takes my breath away. I am so lucky to have you in my life and I promise to always treat you with the love and respect you deserve. I want you to know that you mean everything to me. I will always stand by your side through thick and thin. I will always be here to wipe away your tears to hold your hand and to make you smile. I promise to be your partner in every aspect of life and to make every moment we share together. My love for you is infinite. It knows no bounds and it only grows stronger with each passing day. You are the missing piece of my puzzle and I cannot imagine my life without you. I love you more than words can express and I will always be here for you, no matter what happens. I need you! Now and forever!

Printed by Libri Plureos GmbH in Hamburg,
Germany